America's Leaders

The

SPEAKER

of the House

by Howard Gutner

BLACKBIRCH®
PRESS

THOMSON

GALE

San Diego • Detroit • New York • San Francisco • Cleveland • New Haven, Conn. • Waterville, Maine • London • Munich

LIBRARY OF CONGRESS CATALOGING-IN-PUBLICATION DATA

Gutner, Howard.
  The Speaker of the House / by Howard Gutner.
     v. cm. — (America's leaders series)
Includes index.
Contents: The legislative branch — Leadership in the House of Representatives — Who works with the Speaker? — The whip system — Where does the Speaker of the House work? — A time of crisis — Another time of crisis — The Speaker's day.
  ISBN 1-56711-964-6 (hardback : alk. paper)
  1. United States. Congress. House—Speaker—Juvenile literature. 2. United States. Congress. House—Leadership—Juvenile literature. [1. United States. Congress. House—Speaker.] I. Title. II. Series.

JK1411 .G88 2004
328.73'0762—dc21   2002012886

Table of Contents

The Three Branches

More than 200 years ago, a group of men wrote a document, the U.S. Constitution, which established the American government. The authors of the Constitution divided the government into three separate branches— the legislative branch, the judicial branch, and the executive branch.

The legislative branch was given the power to pass the nation's laws. It was made up of two houses of Congress. One house was the House of Representatives. The other house was the Senate.

The Cannon House of Representatives Building (pictured) in Washington, D.C., houses offices of members of the U.S. House of Representatives.

Some members of the U.S. Senate have offices at the Russell Senate Office Building (pictured) in Washington, D.C.

The judicial branch of government established a system of courts. This branch was given the power to decide whether laws passed by Congress agreed with the principles of the Constitution.

The executive branch was given the power to put the nation's laws into effect and enforce them. The Constitution states that the leader of the executive branch is the president.

All 535 members of Congress can meet together in the U.S. Capitol (pictured) for important events.

Looking at the Legislative Branch

The legislative branch has two parts: the House of Representatives and the Senate. Every state, no matter how small, has U.S. two senators. That means that the Senate has 100 members (2 from each of the 50 states).

The number of representatives that each state has in the House depends on how many people live in the state. States with more people have more representatives than states with fewer people. Today, the House has 435 members, who serve two-year terms. Elections are held in November of even-numbered years, and the representatives take office the following January.

The members of the House choose their own leader. This person is called the Speaker of the House. It is a very important position, because the Speaker's job is to manage the House of Representatives. The Speaker has the power to appoint representatives to the committees that debate and decide key issues. The Speaker must also make sure that the other representatives get their work done.

As head of the House of Representatives, the Speaker appoints other representatives to House committees. Pictured is Speaker of the House in 1990, Thomas Foley (right), accompanied by Senate majority leader George Mitchell (left) and House majority leader Richard Gephardt (center).

A Changing Position

When Congress met for the first time in 1789, the House wanted a leader who would not take sides on issues. For many years, the Speaker of the House took care to be neutral. Speakers did not even vote on bills, even though they were supposed to represent people from their district.

Then, in 1811, a man named Henry Clay became Speaker of the House. At that time, England's navy controlled the Atlantic Ocean. The British told the United States where its ships could sail. This restricted where the United States could trade goods. At the beginning of the 19th century, England also gave money to Native Americans to help them fight settlers in western states such as Ohio and Kentucky.

Henry Clay (pictured) changed the role of Speaker of the House into one of national influence.

For these reasons, Henry Clay wanted Congress to declare war on England. President James Madison, however, did not want to go to war.

This painting shows Speaker of the House Henry Clay (standing, center) addressing the U.S. Senate.

Before and after he became Speaker, Clay spent time with other representatives. He made a point to meet with representatives from western states where Native American uprisings were common. He convinced them that it was time to elect a Speaker who would help the settlers and make American ships safe on the Atlantic. The other representatives were impressed with Clay. On November 4, 1811, they elected him Speaker of the House.

President James Madison (pictured) was persuaded by the Speaker Henry Clay to go to war with England.

When the new Congress met in January, Clay went right to work. He appointed to committees the members of the House who agreed with him about the need for war with England. He was also strict with representatives about the way they behaved when the House was in session. When one member kept falling asleep during a session, Clay told him to either wake up or go home to bed.

Unlike previous Speakers, Henry Clay also voted on bills. In fact, he gave speeches to try and convince other representatives to vote his way on issues. Eventually, he convinced a majority of members, as well as Madison, to go to war with England. On June 12, 1812, the president signed a declaration of war.

By the time Henry Clay left office in 1825, he had changed the way people looked at the position of Speaker of the House. It was no longer a neutral position. It had become a base of power. The Speaker of the House was now someone who could influence national events.

The Speaker's Job Today

Today, the Speaker of the House can have a lot of influence on a president's ability to get laws passed by Congress. If the Speaker agrees with the president on an issue, he can make the passage of laws on that issue much easier for the president. If the Speaker is at odds with the president, however, he can make it very hard for the president to get bills passed.

As his title suggests, the Speaker also gets to decide who may speak when the House of Representatives meets. The speaker has to follow certain guidelines, but this ability gives him a great deal of power.

John McCormack (right) was Speaker of the House in 1968. The Speaker decides which representatives are allowed to speak at meetings.

11

Mr. Lindsey

The Speaker chooses House members to serve on committees. In this photo, persons who are to testify at a committee hearing are being sworn in.

The Speaker also settles disagreements about the guidelines—called parliamentary rules—that tell how debates take place in the House. The Speaker often asks for help from someone called a parliamentarian to try to decide how the rules should be followed.

When the need arises, the Speaker chooses House members to serve on committees. Two of the most important committees are select committees and conference committees. The members of a select committee do special research on certain issues, such as global warming. When they are finished, they write a report for the rest of the House.

A conference committee looks at differences between bills passed by the Senate and bills passed by the House of Representatives. For example, the Senate could pass a bill to spend more money on education. It might be a bit different from a similar bill in the House. The members of the conference committee work to come up with a new version of the bill that will please both the House and Senate.

Any representative in the House can suggest a bill. He or she simply places it in a basket at the side of the Clerk's desk in the House Chamber. The representative's signature must appear on the bill. Then it is assigned a number by the Clerk and given to the right committee by the Speaker. After the bill is reviewed and debated by a number of representatives, it goes to the Committee on Rules.

Florida representative Claude Pepper was chairman of the House Rules Committee in 1968. The Rules Committee reviews all bills proposed in the House.

In 1965, Virginia representative Howard V. Smith (pictured) was chairman of the House Rules Committee. The Speaker of the House appointed him to the position.

The Committee on Rules decides when bills are scheduled for a vote on the floor of the House. The Speaker names the chairperson and the members of this committee. By controlling the membership of the Rules Committee, the speaker influences the kinds of bills that come to the floor for a vote.

Who Can Become Speaker of the House?

After a national election, the entire House votes to select a Speaker. The Democratic and Republican Parties place the name of their candidates in nomination. The candidate must be another representative in the House who has been elected to Congress. Otherwise, there are no special qualifications or requirements for the position. The members of each political party almost always vote for the candidate who represents their party.

In the early 19th century, more than a dozen political parties fought for votes across the United States. No party had a majority of representatives in the House. When Congress met in 1855, for example, the House had to vote 133 times before the members could agree on a Speaker.

Speaker of the House Jim Wright (pictured) held a giant gavel, the symbol of his office, at the opening session of Congress in 1988. The House Democratic majority elected him Speaker.

In 1994, the Republican Party won a majority of seats in the House and was thus entitled to elect the Speaker. They chose Newt Gingrich, pictured here (right) during a TV interview.

Today, there are only two major political parties in the United States. That makes the election of the Speaker fairly easy. For example, if the Democratic Party has more representatives elected to the House than the Republican Party, the Democrats will get to choose the Speaker of the House. If the majority of the representatives are Republican, then the Speaker of the House will be a Republican.

Who Works with the Speaker?

There are 435 members in the House of Representatives. Both the Democrats and the Republicans need to have people who will work closely with the Speaker of the House. They also want to make sure

that the bills that are important to their party have a good chance to be passed.

Republican Louisiana representative Robert Livingston (center) was elected Speaker of the House in 1998. Representatives from both parties must be able to work closely and effectively with the Speaker.

The Majority and Minority Leaders

The majority leader in the House of Representatives is elected every two years. He or she is chosen by the political party that has a majority of members in the House. As a result, the majority leader is always a member of the same political party as the Speaker.

The majority leader works with the Speaker to schedule legislation for House members to vote on. The majority leader also tries to reach the goals of his or her political party. To do this, he or she might meet with other members of the party to find out what they think about a certain bill. The majority leader then works with these representatives to support or try to defeat bills that come up for a vote.

Republican Dick Armey (at podium), the House majority leader in 2002, addressed reporters at a news conference that year. The majority leader always belongs to the same political party as the Speaker.

18

The political party that does not have a majority of representatives in the House elects a minority leader who speaks for the minority party. He or she tries to think of ways that can help the minority party get their ideas across. One way is to come up with bills that offer an alternative to the bills of the majority party.

Both the Speaker and the majority leader try to find ways to help other representatives in their party. For example, they may schedule a vote at a convenient time for a representative. They also

In late 2002, Democrat Nancy Pelosi of California (pictured) was the first woman elected House minority leader. The minority and majority leaders head their respective parties in Congress.

may speak to support a representative's bill. Sometimes they help the representative get re-elected to Congress when his or her term is up. When they help members of their party in these ways, they are able to build coalitions and keep the party united.

The Whip System

When the House of Representatives meets for the first time after an election, each party elects a whip. The whip tries to get all the members of the party to vote the same way. If a bill that is up for a vote has been brought to the House by a Republican, for example, the Republican whip's job is to try to get other Republicans to vote for it. The whips also let representatives know when an important vote will come up, and keep them informed about the different committees and their work.

The whip of the majority party is called the majority whip. He or she works closely with the Speaker of the House and the majority leader to come up with ideas and plans that will help pass bills that are important to their party.

Republican representative Tom DeLay (pictured, center) was the majority whip in 2000. Whips work to get members of their parties to vote together on important bills.

Where Does the Speaker of the House Work?

The office of the Speaker of the House is in the U.S. Capitol in Washington, D.C. The building is divided into five levels. The office of the Speaker is located on the second floor. This floor also holds the rooms where the House of Representatives and the Senate meet.

In and Out of Washington

Because the Speaker of the House is an important leader, he meets often with the president. These meetings may take place in the president's main working area—the Oval Office in the White House.

The Speaker of the House's office is in the Capitol in Washington, D.C. Carl Albert, pictured here at his desk in that office, was Speaker when he retired in 1977.

The Speaker also works with other members of the House of Representatives in their offices. These offices are housed in three buildings that are located just south of the Capitol.

Besides the office at the Capitol, the Speaker of the House usually has another office in his or her own state's district. On trips home, the Speaker meets local people at the district office and listens to their ideas and concerns.

A Time of Crisis

In the 1970s, oil and gas prices in the United States were skyrocketing. Supplies were being choked off by the producers in the Middle East. There were long lines at gas stations as people waited to fill up their gas tanks.

When Democrat Jimmy Carter became president in 1976, he knew something had to be done. He wanted to place limits on gas prices. He also wanted people to be careful about how much energy they used. Carter asked Speaker Thomas "Tip" O'Neill to help him get new laws passed by the House that would accomplish these goals.

Carter's energy bill called for a special tax on people who bought cars that did not get good gas mileage. Energy companies that started programs to research the development of solar and wind power would get special tax credits. Also, companies that made appliances like

In the 1970s, Speaker Thomas "Tip" O'Neill (pictured) created a new type of committee in order to help President Jimmy Carter get a landmark energy bill passed.

microwave ovens would have to make products that ran on less electricity.

Carter wanted his energy bill passed by Congress before December 31, 1977. Tip O'Neill did everything he could to help the president meet this deadline in the House. First, he established an ad hoc Committee on Energy. An ad hoc committee is one that is formed to deal with a specific and important problem. This kind of committee had never been formed in the House of Representatives before. He also set firm deadlines for representatives to debate and vote on parts of the bill.

The Senate, however, split Carter's bill into six separate bills. House Republicans then came up with a substitute bill. It was similar to the president's but much less strict. When it came to a vote, however, the House would not pass it. Finally, a conference committee worked out a compromise bill between the one in the House and the one in the Senate. It passed the House by one vote, 207-206.

Most of the taxes Carter wanted were gone from the bill. Although companies would have to make more efficient appliances, the bill gave them more time to do so. Nevertheless, this compromise bill was a landmark. It paved the way for many conservation rules that are still in use today.

Another Time of Crisis

During the 1950s, civil rights bills were always defeated in Congress. This was because representatives from the South controlled most of the committees in the House. The chair of the Rules Committee, Howard Smith of Virginia, used his power as chairman to stop bills. Any bill that would improve the conditions of African Americans, for example, would never reach the floor for a vote.

In the 1960s, Speaker Sam Rayburn, pictured here calling the House to order, was able to get civil rights laws passed by appointing new members to the Rules Committee.

Civil rights activists often marched in Washington, D.C., in the 1960s. Until Speaker Sam Rayburn used his authority to intervene in 1961, however, the House Rules Committee had blocked all attempts to pass a civil rights bill.

In 1960, John F. Kennedy, a Democrat, was elected president. He had many civil rights bills that he wanted Congress to pass. Kennedy asked Sam Rayburn, the Speaker of the House, to help him get his bills passed by Congress. Every time Rayburn tried to get a civil rights bill to the floor for a vote, though, he was stopped by Howard Smith and the Rules Committee.

Rayburn soon understood that he had to do something drastic. He needed to change the Rules Committee itself. In 1961, Rayburn was successful. In a very close vote (217-212) the House passed a bill that Rayburn had introduced. It allowed him, as Speaker, to appoint three new members to the Rules Committee. As a result, he broke Howard Smith's hold on the Committee, and civil rights bills finally made it to the floor for a vote.

The Speaker's Day

The Speaker of the House is a busy person whose days are filled with meetings and public appearances. Here is what a day might be like for the Speaker of the House.

6:00 AM   Wake, shower, watch television news, and scan several newspapers

6:30 AM   Eat breakfast

7:00 AM   At work in the Capitol. Meet with assistants; check E-mail messages

8:00 AM   Meeting with the majority leader and the majority whip to discuss upcoming bills that are coming to the floor of the House for a vote

10:00 AM   Work on a speech in support of a spending bill that will give more benefits to people who have lost their jobs

11:00 AM   Interview with host of national radio talk show

1:00 PM   Working lunch with the minority whip in the Capitol dining room to hear how the minority party feels about the benefits bill

2:30 PM   Meeting with the president in the Oval Office to talk about changes the president wants to make in the benefits bill

As the most powerful member of the House, the Speaker works closely with the president. In this photo, Speaker Carl Albert (left) discusses issues with President Richard Nixon in 1971.

4:00 PM	Return to the office in the Capitol to meet with a group of people from the Speaker's home state
5:30 PM	Review a report from a select committee about cleaning up several pollution sites in the southwestern United States
6:30 PM	Return home. Eat dinner and watch evening news
7:30 PM	Handle pressing paperwork
8:30 PM	Phone call from the majority leader. Discuss upcoming vote on the benefits bill and how much party support the Speaker can expect
9:30 PM	Phone call to the majority whip to ask for a report to be delivered in the morning
10:30 PM	Bed

Fascinating Facts

Sam Rayburn served the longest term in office as Speaker of the House. He was Speaker for 17 years, from 1940–1947, and then again from 1949–1953 and 1955–1961.

Sam Rayburn

James K. Polk was the only Speaker of the House who went on to become president of the United States. Polk served as Speaker from 1835–1839, during the terms of Presidents Andrew Jackson and Martin Van Buren. He was elected president in 1845 and served one four-year term in office.

James K. Polk

Theodore M. Pomeroy served the shortest term in office as Speaker of the House. He was elected Speaker on March 3, 1869, and served only one day. He resigned the position the following day and was succeeded by **James G. Blaine.**

In 1855, representatives had to vote 133 times before they could agree on a Speaker of the House. They finally elected **Nathaniel P. Banks** of the American Party. Banks served for only two years. This was the only time the American Party held the Speaker position in the House.

Nathaniel P. Banks

Two Speakers of the House, **Frederick Muhlenberg** and **Joseph W. Martin Jr.**, also served non-consecutive terms as Speaker. Muhlenberg was Speaker from 1789–1791, and from 1793–1795. Martin held the position from 1947–1949, and again from 1953–1955.

Joseph W. Martin Jr. (pictured) was one of only two Speakers of the House to serve non-consecutive terms.

Glossary

ad hoc committee—a committee that is formed to deal with a specific and important problem

bill—the draft of a proposed law

census—an official count of the people who live in a country or district

coalition—a group of politicians that gather together to support a bill or special cause

conference committee—a committee that helps work out differences between bills passed by the House of Representatives and those passed by the Senate

Congress—the legislative branch of government, composed of the Senate and the House of Representatives

constituent—a person who has the power to vote and elect someone to a political office

Constitution—the document that established the United States government that contains the principles and laws of the nation

legislation—the making of laws

majority leader—the leader of the party that controls the house, who is chosen by the other party members

minority leader—the leader of the party that does not control the house, who is chosen by other party members

nominate—to name someone as a candidate for a political office

Oval Office—the office in the West Wing of the White House from which the president works and meets with important people such as the Speaker of the House

parliamentary rules—rules, based on acceptable language and actions, that are used during a debate in the House of Representatives or in other government bodies that consider bills

select committee—a committee that directs special investigations into specific issues

treaty—an agreement between two nations

whip—a party member who is appointed to keep other party members together for united action

For More Information

Publications

Feinberg, Barbara Silberdick, *The National Government.* New York. Franklin Watts, 1993.

Fish, Bruce and Becky Durost. *The Speaker of the House of Representatives.* Philadelphia. Chelsea House, 2001.

31

Index